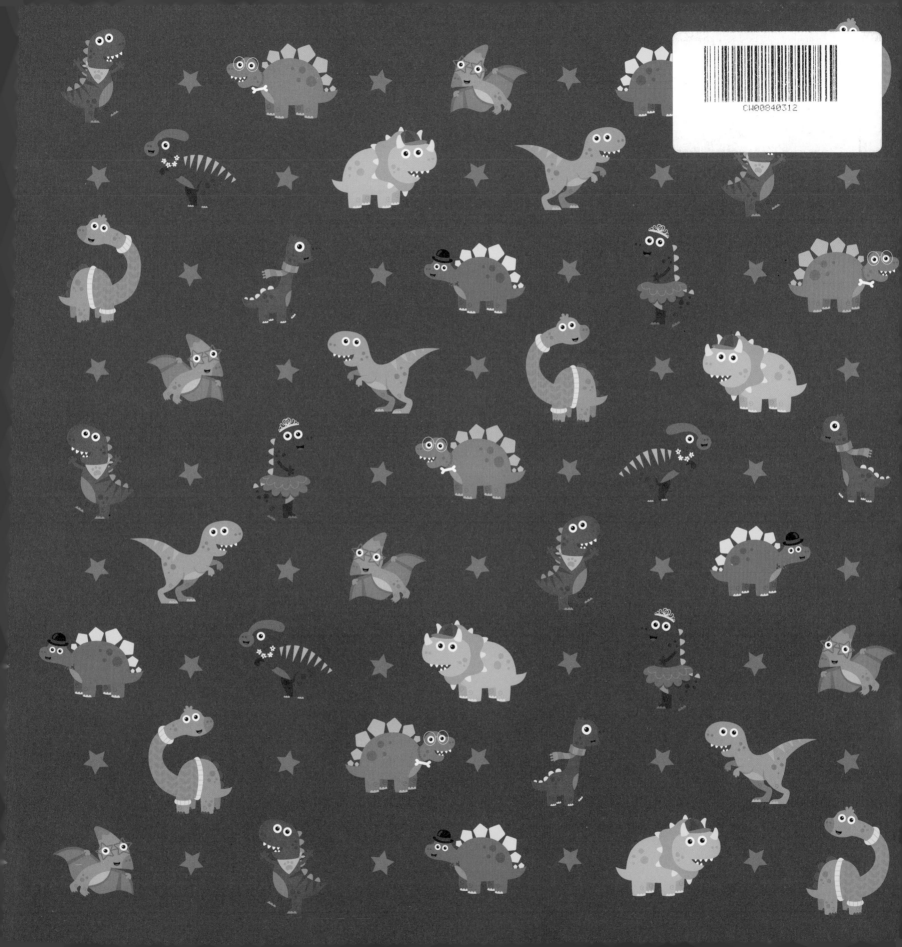

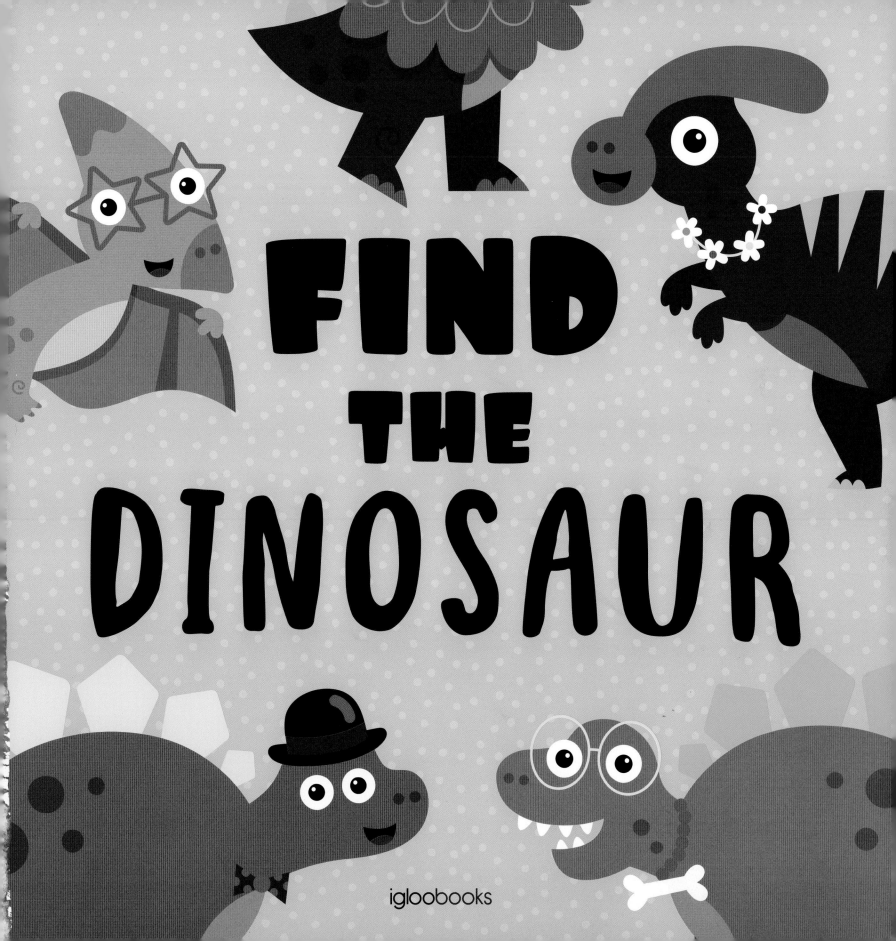

FIND THE DINOSAUR

igloobooks

MEET THE DINOSAURS!

Ten little dinosaurs are hiding on every page in this fun book! Read the profiles below to learn all about each of the roar-some creatures. Then, look carefully at the scenes to try and find where they are all hiding. The answers are at the back of the book so you can check your searching skills.

TWINKLE

LOVES:
Ballet dancing

FAVOURITE OUTFIT:
Pink tutu

BEST DANCE MOVE:
The twirl-stomp

DOTTY

FAVOURITE GAME:
Hide-and-stomp

ALWAYS WEARS:
Snuggly jumper

FAVOURITE BOOK:
The thesaurus

REX

FAVOURITE MEAL:
Afternoon tea-rex

KNOWN FOR:
Tyranno-snoring loudly

ALWAYS WEARS:
Green neckerchief

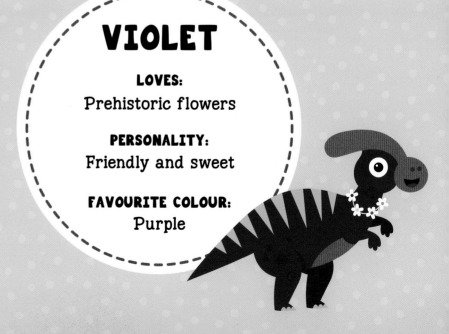

VIOLET

LOVES:
Prehistoric flowers

PERSONALITY:
Friendly and sweet

FAVOURITE COLOUR:
Purple

STEVE

ALWAYS WEARS:
Bowler hat

HOBBY:
Sings in the
tyranno-chorus

LOVES:
Bow ties

SPIKE

DISLIKES:
Dino-chores

KNOWN FOR:
Can't tricera-stop
telling jokes

ALWAYS WEARS:
Red hat

TILLY

SECRET TALENT:
Pter-rific at tap dance

HALLOWEEN COSTUME:
Terror-dactyl

MOST-LOVED ACCESSORY:
Star glasses

LEO

KNOWN FOR:
Being super fast

BIGGEST GOAL:
To be a famous velocir-actor

FAVOURITE FOOD:
Rock cake

SPOT

FAVOURITE THING TO DO:
Shop at dino-stores

MOST-EATEN SNACK:
Volcano ice cream

PERSONALITY:
Always cheerful

DANI

FAVOURITE ACCESSORY:
Cosy scarf

SECRET TALENT:
Cave painting

FAVOURITE COLOUR:
Blue

FOSSIL FUN

There's so much to see at the Dino Museum!
Can you find all ten dinosaur friends?

CAN YOU SPOT THE RED FOSSIL?

JURASSIC JUNGLE

The noisy jungle is full of ROARS and SQUAWKS!
Where are all ten dinos hiding?

CAN YOU SPOT THE YELLOW MUSHROOM?

DINO SPORTS

The dinos love joining the fun at sports day!
Can you spot where all ten are hiding?

CAN YOU SPOT THE PURPLE TENNIS BALL?

SEASIDE STOMP

The dinos love sunbathing and splashing in the sea.
All ten are hiding at the seaside. Can you spot where?

CAN YOU SPOT THE YELLOW BIRD?

CANDYLAND CRUNCH

The dinosaurs love to MUNCH and CRUNCH on sweets!
Can you spot all ten dinosaurs in the scene?

CAN YOU SPOT THE PINK COOKIE?

PREHISTORIC PLANET

The dinos love exploring faraway planets! Zoom among
the astronauts and aliens to find all ten dinos.

CAN YOU SPOT THE GREEN MOON?

CHOC-OSAURS

The dinos have sneaked into this chocolate factory hoping for a yummy snack! Can you spot all ten?

CAN YOU SPOT THE JAR OF SWEETS?

DINO DISCO

It's party time! This fancy-dress party is perfect for dancing dinos. Can you find all ten?

CAN YOU SPOT THE RED MUSIC NOTE?

TOY-REX TROUBLE

Look at all the toys in this busy shop!
Can you see all ten dinos hiding here, too?

CAN YOU SPOT THE RED GUITAR?

AMAZING ANIMALS

The farmyard is full of noisy animals, big and small.
Look closely! There are ten dinosaurs to find.

CAN YOU SPOT THE PURPLE SQUIRREL?

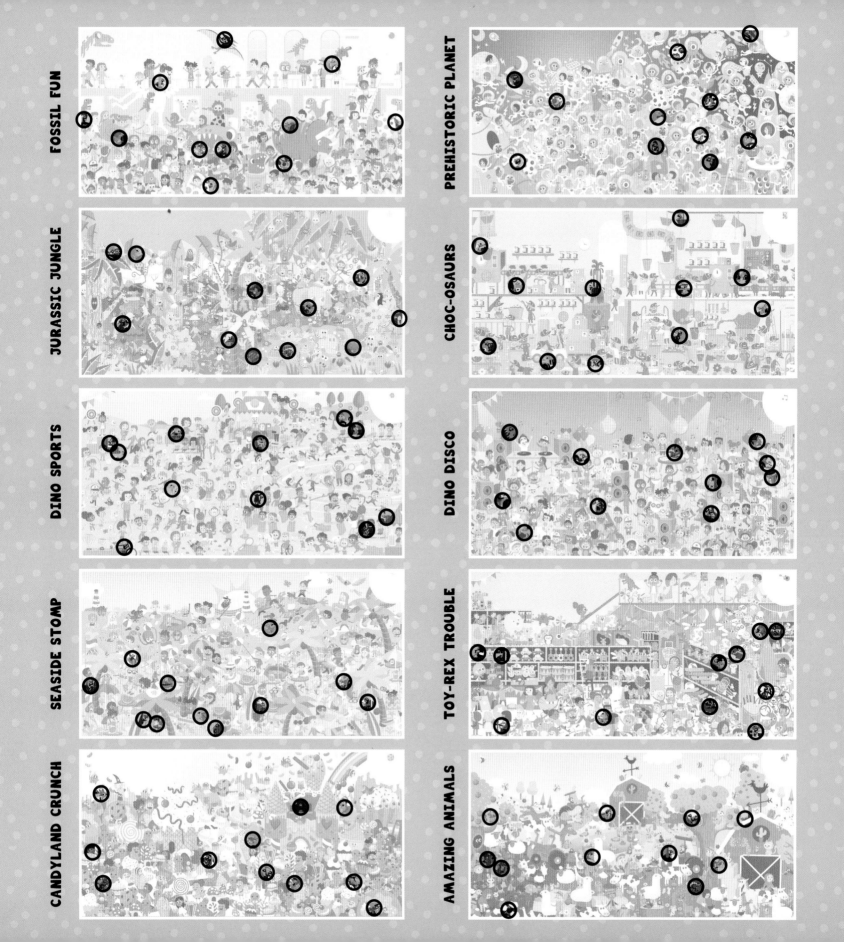

FOSSIL FUN

PREHISTORIC PLANET

JURASSIC JUNGLE

CHOC-OSAURS

DINO SPORTS

DINO DISCO

SEASIDE STOMP

TOY-REX TROUBLE

CANDYLAND CRUNCH

AMAZING ANIMALS